DYLAN'S AMAZING DINOSAURS

THE TYRANNOSAURUS REX

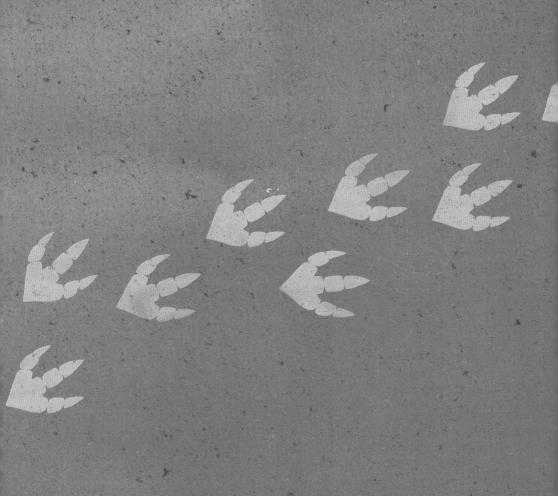

For Xander and Lily, with love x – E.H.

For George Bear, my wonderful nephew – D.T.

SIMON & SCHUSTER
First published in Great Britain in 2014. This special edition published in 2021 by Simon & Schuster Uk Ltd • 1st Floor, 222 Gray's Inn Road, London, WC1X 8HB • Text copyright © 2014 E.T. Harper • Illustrations copyright © 2014 Dan Taylor • The right of E.T. Harper and Dan Taylor to be identified as the author and illustrator of this work has been asserted by them in accordance with the Copyright, Designs and Patents Act, 1988 • All rights reserved, including the right of reproduction in whole or in part in any form • A CIP catalogue record for this book is available from the British Library upon request • ISBN: 978-1-4711-4419-6 • Printed in China • 10 9 8 7 6 5 4 3 2 1

DYLAN'S AMAZING DINOSAURS

THE TYRANNOSAURUS REX

E.T. HARPER AND DAN TAYLOR

SIMON & SCHUSTER
London   New York   Sydney   Toronto   New Delhi

Dylan had an incredible tree house. It was full of
fantastic things, and the most fantastic of all were
Grandpa Fossil's magic Dinosaur Journal and . . .

Keep Out!

WINGS, Dylan's toy pterodactyl!
He came to life whenever Dylan opened the journal and they
flew off on amazing adventures together to make awesome
dinosaur discoveries.

'Hey, Wings!' Dylan called as he flung the journal open.
'I wonder what discovery we'll make today?'

Fact File

Bite: Three times as strong as a great white shark

Size: 12 metres (as long as a bus and the weight of two elephants)

Habitat: Forests, plains and swamps

Extraordinary feature: Teeth the size of a man's hand.

Number of teeth: ....

Tyrannosaurus rex
↓

'Hmm . . .' Dylan said. 'So that's our mission, Wings!
We need to find out how many teeth the T. rex had!'

At the mention of a Dino Mission, Wings leapt to life,
shook out his wings and swooped down from the shelf.

'Let's go, let's soar, off to the land
where the dinosaurs roar!' Dylan shouted.

Dylan grabbed his binoculars as they flew over Roar Island.

'Look, Wings! A Hadrosaur, a Stegosaurus, a Triceratops and there's a TYRANNOSAURUS!

Quick, let's land before we lose it!'

Dylan hopped off Wings, and inched forward to get
a better look at the gigantic creature. But he got too close . . .

ROOOAAAARRRGGHHHHH!

The T. rex caught Dylan's scent in his nostrils. It turned its giant head, and bared its GINORMOUS gnashers.

'Yikes!' yelped Dylan, as he started
to run. 'Are those teeth for real?'

The ground shook beneath his feet. 'Fly over the T. rex Wings!'
shouted Dylan desperately. 'We have to confuse it.'

Dylan ran as fast as he could but the T. rex was still coming.

Dylan dived, panting, into a hollow log. 'Phew, that was close!'

The T. rex stopped. And sniffed.

The ferocious beast opened its jaws so wide that Dylan could feel its disgusting, meaty breath on his face.

Dylan needed a plan, and fast!

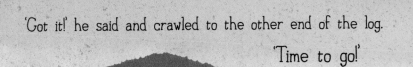

'Got it!' he said and crawled to the other end of the log.

'Time to go!'

Dylan shot out of the log just as the
Tyrannosaurus sunk its teeth in.

The giant dino shook its head and growled in frustration. Dylan's plan had worked – the T. rex's teeth were stuck! Dylan dived into a nearby swamp and watched the T. rex try to get its teeth free from the log.

Finally, with an earth-shaking snarl, the T. rex freed its fearsome fangs. Turning its head, it hunted for its Dylan-shaped dinner.

Sinking lower into the swamp, Dylan disguised his scent with stinky mud, pulled grass over his head and hid. He held his breath as the Tyrannosaur's beady eyes and super-sensitive snout scanned over him.

It felt like forever but at last the T. rex caught sight of
a tastier-looking dinosaur dinner and charged off.

Dylan searched the sky for Wings. 'Help!
The T. rex has gone . . . but now I'm really sinking!'

Just in time, Wings swooped down and pulled Dylan out.

'Wow! Thanks, Wings!' called Dylan. 'Now let's get that missing information before the T. rex comes back for pudding!'

Wings dropped him by the log.
'Its teeth are HUGE!' exclaimed Dylan as he started to count the holes.

'One, two, three . . .
        fifty-six, fifty-seven . . .
                FIFTY-EIGHT TEETH!
                        That T. rex has the meanest bite EVER!

'Dino Mission accomplished, Wings! Let's fly!'

Dylan jumped on the pterodactyl's back and they took off for home.

Back in the tree house Dylan grabbed an apple and took a huge bite, heaving the magic Dinosaur Journal onto his lap.

He scribbled the number 58 into the T. rex fact file.

'Hey Wings, look!' Dylan held out his apple.
'I can count my teeth too!'

Wings smiled and jumped back on to the tree house shelf,
ready and waiting for their next adventure.

Look out for more amazing adventures
with Dylan and Wings!

Out now -
The Stegosaurus

Coming soon -
The Spinosaurus
The Triceratops